MIGHTY JACK and ZITA THE SPACEGIRL

MIGHTY JACK and ZITA THE SPACEGIRL

BEN HATKE

Color by Alex Campbell
and Hilary Sycamore

:01

First Second

New York

ZITA THE SPACEGIRL

The lives of Zita and her friend Joseph were changed forever the day they found a red button in a crater in the grassy hillside behind their houses. One press of the button and Zita was on her way to becoming an interplanetary adventurer. It's a life that has brought her both fame and infamy on worlds beyond Earth.

After overthrowing and destroying a corrupt prison planet, Zita and Joseph found themselves back on Earth. Joseph, now a mechanical expert with an alien cape, was content to resume his old life. But, unable to return to her interstellar adventures without a working jump crystal, Zita felt stranded on her home planet. At least she was joined by her friends—the roguish inventor Piper, the circus ring mistress Lady Madrigal, the giant mouse Pizzicato, the gentle Strong-Strong, and the robots One and Robot Randy. For two years they've stayed hidden in the everyday world.

But recently Piper and Madrigal, stirred by rumors of danger approaching Earth, have driven off in search of answers, and a way back to the stars...

MIGHTY JACK

The lives of Jack and his sister, Maddy, turned upside down the day they took home a box of otherworldly seeds from the flea market near their rural home. The seeds they planted sprouted into a vast garden full of alien flora that brought danger and excitement into their backyard, along with new friends: Lilly, a precocious neighbor girl with a knack for swordsmanship, and Phelix, a dragon with whom Maddy developed a mysterious psychic connection.

But their adventures took a turn when Maddy was kidnapped by an ogre and dragged through a portal in the garden into a pocket dimension ruled by a trio of horrible giants. Jack and Lilly embarked on a desperate rescue mission to the Inbetween and returned forever altered—Jack imbued with powers from the garden's plants, and Lilly taking up the mantle of Goblin King and the ability to shift between human and goblin form. The three young heroes carried on with their lives, burdened with the knowledge that there are other, stranger worlds beyond their own.

And then, one autumn night, Jack and Lilly met Zita the Spacegirl and adventure called again...

NO! PLEASE NO!

23

IT'S THE THING I MISSED MOST OUT THERE!

THERE'S NOTHING LIKE IT ON OTHER PLANETS!

CAN WE GET IT?

for SHOPPIN

FOOD WAL

PLONK.

HEY NOW! THIS WASN'T ON THE LIST.

MOM! IT'S JUST PEANUT BUTTER!

BOOP!

JACK, WE'RE ALREADY WAY OVER BUDGET.

MOM! WE HAVE CIVIL WAR GOLD!

OH!

I'VE GOT SOMETHING THAT MIGHT HELP.

DIG DIG.

45

AND THEN I SAID TO SEVEN—

SMOOCH ♥ THE ROBOT

SHE'S NOT TRYING TO, YOU KNOW—

SHE JUST DOESN'T GET TO TALK ABOUT THAT STUFF MUCH.

WAIT—

YOU THINK I'M JEALOUS?

ARE YOU?

WE'RE SUPPOSED TO BE PREPARING FOR SOME GREAT DANGER, RIGHT?

ISN'T THAT WHAT YOUR FRIEND PIPER SAID? BEFORE HE LEFT?

WE'VE GOT TIME, THOUGH.

THE DOORWAY TO THE INBETWEEN IS CLOSED. THAT'S WHAT YOU AND JACK SAID. IT DOESN'T EVEN EXIST ON OUR SIDE.

WHATEVER "DANGER" PIPER SENSED, IT CAN'T BE THAT CLOSE.

RIGHT?

...

THEY'RE COMING!

WE'RE OUT OF TIME!

BOOM!

DOP!

THE LADY HAS TOLD ME WHAT IS AT STAKE.

I CAN CREATE A WYRMHOLE FOR YOU. SAFE PASSAGE TO THE INBETWEEN.

I GUESS WE'RE THE ONLY ONES WHO MADE IT THROUGH.

WE'LL MAKE IT WORK.

WE SHOULD START LOOKING—

GET DOWN!

aak!

BOOM! BOOM! BOOM!

YIKES.

THERE'S MORE OF THEM THAN I EXPECTED.

THAT'S THE DOOR TO THE ELF WORLD?

IT'S DARK.

WHAT HAPPENED HERE?

HEH HEH HEHH...

VROM!

THIS PLACE LOOKS—

DEAD.

IT'S A DEAD WORLD.

NO WONDER THE GIANTS WANT EARTH.

NO. IT'S NOT JUST THIS DEAD PLACE BUT AN ANCIENT HATRED MY PEOPLE HAVE FOR YOURS.

IT'S TIME TO PUT THAT HATRED TO REST.

WELL?

A DAY'S JOURNEY FROM HERE, THERE IS A PLACE CALLED THE ELDERS' GATE.

IT IS A TREASURE ROOM THAT HOLDS MY EMPEROR'S GREATEST SECRET.

HIS HEART.

HE KEEPS IT LOCKED AWAY SO THAT, ON THE FIELD OF BATTLE, HE CANNOT BE KILLED. IT IS BOTH HIS GREATEST STRENGTH AND HIS GREATEST WEAKNESS.

I WILL LEAD YOU THERE.

YOU WILL HOLD THE EMPEROR'S HEART OVER A FLAME, AND HE AND ALL THE GIANTS WILL RUSH BACK HERE TO STOP YOU. AS LONG AS YOU HAVE THE HEART, THE GIANTS WILL BE AT YOUR MERCY.

JUST A FEW MORE AND WE'LL BE THROUGH!

HAROOOOOO!

AROOOOOOO!

...

WOW.

BLOW IT! NOW!

AYE AYE, CHIEF!

FSSS!

LAST SUMMER, WHEN WE HAD THE GARDEN, BEFORE MADDY WAS TAKEN...

I STOLE SEEDS. GREW A GARDEN OF MY OWN IN MY BASEMENT.

THEN, AFTER MADDY, I TORE IT ALL UP. EXCEPT...

ONE SEED HAD GROWN INTO A SMALL DOOR.

I KEPT THE DOOR HIDDEN, BUT I THOUGHT ABOUT IT EVERY DAY. ALL WINTER.

I THOUGHT ABOUT SEEING MY GOBLINS AGAIN.

144

I THINK YOU DID THE RIGHT THING. THE GOBLINS NEEDED YOU.

I THINK...

I THINK NO MATTER HOW HARD YOU TRY TO DO RIGHT, THINGS WILL GO WRONG SOMEHOW.

BUT IT'S WORSE IF YOU STOP TRYING.

MAYBE —
UM, OH.

Z.

Z.

KEY.

OH—

RIGHT.

149

153

CLANG!
SWIFF!

THERE'S — NH!
THERE'S TOO MANY
OF THESE
THINGS!

WE'RE BEING
DRIVEN BACK!
DRIVEN TO THE —

RELEASE!

LOOK
OUT!

WE'RE THROUGH.

EXCELLENT.

WHAT DO YOU SAY, OLD FRIEND?

SIGH.

MY LORD!

EH?

WHAT IS IT?

WHAT ARE WE GOING TO DO?

SEARCH AROUND. MAYBE THERE'S SOMETHING WE CAN USE TO GET OUT.

AND THEN WHAT?

WE'LL STILL BE TRAPPED ON THIS WORLD!

I DON'T KNOW!

I DON'T KNOW, OKAY? SHOULD WE JUST GIVE UP?

ZITA'S RIGHT. IT'S WORSE IF WE STOP TRYING.

SINK

THEY'RE DYING.

W—WE FAILED.

OOG.

CHIEF?

BOOM BOOM CRASH

aah!

C'MON, C'MON!

TEK TEK TEK!

IT'S TIME TO GO HOME, YEAH?

Y-YEAH.

IT'S JUST—

I NEVER THOUGHT I'D BE BACK HERE. THAT LITTLE BOT THERE IS THE PILOT.

SHE TOOK MY PLACE AT THE CONTROLS OF THIS MECH. SHE SACRIFICED HERSELF FOR ME.

TWITCH.

MY, UH, MY LORD?

WHAT IS IT?

THIS IS A MORE... FORMIDABLE FORCE THAN WE EXPECTED.

THEY HAVE A DRAGON.

WHAT DO WE DO?

WE CHARGE!

SHOW-OFF.

OKAY, TEN.

YOU CAN DO YOUR THING.

SMEK.

I'VE NEVER BEEN SO PROUD!

DRAGNON HUG!

Y-YES.

HA HA!

NICE SPEECH.

244

WE'RE NOT GOING BACK.

BUT!!

GONNA STAY ON EARTH FOR THE NEXT LITTLE WHILE.

GET A LITTLE THATCHED ROOF COTTAGE. OR a BOAT!

BUT-!

BUT I CAN'T STAY HERE!

I KNOW.

HERE.

MY SHIP IS YOURS NOW.

BUT!

I ALREADY HAVE a SHIP.

JACK, I CAN'T BELIEVE I'M SAYING THIS,

BUT—

YOU SHOULD GO.

IT'S... OTHER **WORLDS**. I'D BE A POOR MOTHER IF I HELD YOU BACK.

BUT IT'S NOT YOU. I MEAN, NOT JUST YOU.

THE DOORWAY, IT'S IN MY BACKYARD. IT'S CLOSED ON OUR SIDE, BUT OVER THERE, IN THE INBETWEEN...

SIGH.

THAP!

THAT'S GOOD!

NOW CARRY THE ONE.

THE ORIGIN AND EVOLUTION OF
MIGHTY JACK

As best I can remember, I started working on the beginnings of the story that would become *Mighty Jack* in 2006. That's right, I started working on Jack's story *ten years* before the first book was released. Some stories arrive all in a rush; others grow more slowly. I think this story needed a decade to develop.

At that time, my family lived in a tiny little box of a house just a stone's throw from the Shenandoah River. I remember I had just moved my drawing board out of our gloomy, cinderblock basement and into a sunny upstairs room with a window that looked right out over our garden. My wife had planted the garden, and in the steamy Virginia summer it had grown into a scrappy, tangled beast of a thing. I was doing mostly freelance design work at the time, but the garden was where my eyes turned when I daydreamed.

Ten years!

Ten years of development means that the story went through a lot of changes, particularly in its visual development and character design. (Maddy, for instance, started out as a pig-tailed six-year-old!) Of course, throughout those ten years I was also developing the stories of a certain spacegirl, often in the very same notebooks. Looking back, the intersection of those stories' worlds seems inevitable.

Here, then, on the following pages, is a look at how the characters, creatures, and world of Mighty Jack, and the world of Zita the Spacegirl, have changed through the years . . .

VEGGIE
THAT BRINGS
THINGS

UM, EXCUSE ME...

SNUFFLE · SNUFF ·

eh?

HM? OH, I SEE...

AND WHO MIGHT YOU BE?

SPEAK UP, NOW LAD!

MY NAME'S JACK, AND, UM, THIS - THIS IS MY GARDEN.

OH, I SEE! DID YOU KNOW THAT YOU'VE PLANTED WORMWEED HERE? IT'S QUITE RARE, BUT WE DRAGONS CAN'T RESIST IT!

Jack

Lilly

Maddy

ACKNOWLEDGMENTS

It feels like I worked on this book all over the world.

I began drawing the layouts during a surprise blizzard that trapped me, for one perfect, silent day, in a little cabin outside of Portland, Maine. (Thanks, Julia Colvin and Deanne Gouzie!)

I drew a couple of the early pages, surrounded by some of my Very Best Artist Friends, in a lodge outside of Juneau, Alaska. (Thanks Pat Race and co.!)

I drew more of the early pages in my own little studio, next to the rambly farmhouse in the Shenandoah Valley that I call home. (Thanks, dear Anna! And Angelica and Zita and Julia and Ronia and Ida and Pepper! [Pepper's the dog.])

But I drew the bulk of the pages for this book in the village of Gravagna Montale, way up in the Apennine Mountains in Italy. I have tremendous gratitude for all the people of the village who showed me such kindness and interest, particularly Teresa, Sara, Carla, "Galileo," Paulo, Other Paulo, and Mafalda.

Thanks to everyone who read the first inks, particularly Andy O'Neill, who pointed out some places where the action was hard to follow. Oh, and another big thank-you to my daughter Zita, because she gave me some very good advice about the ending.

And, of course, thanks to my agent, Judy Hansen, my publisher, Mark Seigel, and my lovely editor, Calista Brill. Oh, and big bonus thanks to my interim editor, Rachel Stark, and a sage nod of the head to my copyeditor, Kat Kopit, who's been watching over my work since the first Zita book.

And, lastly, thanks to cousins Flavia and Ida Bertolini, keepers of the bright yellow house in Gravagna, whose peaceful veranda I'm sitting on right now as I write these acknowledgments.

First Second

Copyright © 2019 by Ben Hatke
Published by First Second
First Second is an imprint of Roaring Brook Press,
a division of Holtzbrinck Publishing
Holdings Limited Partnership
120 Broadway, New York, NY 10271

Don't miss your next favorite book from First Second!
For the latest updates go to firstsecondnewsletter.com and sign up for our enewsletter.

Library of Congress Control Number: 2018953659

Hardcover ISBN: 978-1-250-19172-4
Paperback ISBN: 978-1-250-19173-1

Our books may be purchased in bulk for promotional, educational, or business use. Please contact your
local bookseller or the Macmillan Corporate and Premium Sales Department at (800) 221-7945 ext. 5442
or by email at MacmillanSpecialMarkets@macmillan.com.

FIRST

EDITION

First edition, 2019
Edited by Calista Brill and Rachel Stark
Book design by Andrew Arnold and Joyana McDiarmid
Colors by Alex Campbell and Hilary Sycamore of Sky Blue Ink
Printed in Canada by TC Transcontinental Printing

Penciled in light blue or light red colored pencils (Crayola or Giotto Supermina). Inked on laser printer paper with Sakura
Pigma Microns and Pentel Pocket Brush Pens. Colored digitally in Photoshop.

Hardcover: 10 9 8 7 6 5 4 3 2 1
Paperback: 10 9 8 7 6 5 4 3 2